THE ZACK FILES

My Grandma, Major-League Slugger

LETTERS TO DAN GREENBURG
ABOUT THE ZACK FILES:

From a mother in New York, NY: "Just wanted to let you know that it was THE ZACK FILES that made my son discover the joy of reading...I tried everything to get him interested...THE ZACK FILES turned my son into a reader overnight. Now he complains when he's out of books!"

From a boy named Toby in New York, NY: "The reason why I like your books is because you explain things that no other writer would even dream of explaining to kids."

From Tara in Floral Park, NY: "When I read your books I felt like I was in the book with you. We love your books!"

From a teacher in West Chester, PA: "I cannot thank you enough for writing such a fantastic series."

From Max in Old Bridge, NJ: "I wasn't such a great reader until I discovered your books."

From Monica in Burbank, IL: "I read almost all of your books and I loved the ones I read. I'm a big fan! *I'm Out of My Body, Please Leave a Message.* That's a funny title. It makes me think of it being the best book in the world."

From three mothers in Toronto: "You have managed to take three boys and unlock the world of reading. In January they could best be characterized as boys who 'read only under duress.' Now these same guys are similar in that they are motivated to READ."

From Stephanie in Hastings, NY: "If someone didn't like your books that would be crazy."

From Dana in Floral Park, NY: "I really LOVE I mean LOVE your books. I read them a million times. I wish I could buy more. They are so good and so funny."

From a teacher in Pelham, NH: "My students are thoroughly enjoying [THE ZACK FILES]. Some are reading a book a night."

From Madeleine in Hastings, NY: "I love your books...I hope you keep making many more Zack Files."

My Grandma, Major-League Slugger

By Dan Greenburg

Illustrated by Jack E. Davis

GROSSET & DUNLAP • NEW YORK

For Judith, and for the real Zack,
with love—D.G.

For technical assistance
I would like to thank my son Zack,
who knows more about baseball
than anybody in the world.

I'd like to thank my editor
Jane O'Connor, who makes the process
of writing and revising so much fun,
and without whom
these books would not exist.

I also want to thank
Emily Sollinger and Tui Sutherland
for their terrific ideas.

Text copyright © 2001 by Dan Greenburg. Illustrations copyright © 2001 by Jack E. Davis. All rights reserved. Published by Grosset & Dunlap, a division of Penguin Putnam Books for Young Readers, New York. GROSSET & DUNLAP and THE ZACK FILES are trademarks of Penguin Putnam Inc. Published simultaneously in Canada. Printed in the U.S.A.

Library of Congress Cataloging-in-Publication Data
Greenburg, Dan.
    My Grandma, major-league slugger / by Dan Greenburg ; illustrated by Jack E. Davis.
        p. cm. — (The Zack files ; 24)
    Summary: When magic enables Zack's eighty-eight-year-old grandmother to become a terrific batter, she ends up playing in a Chicago White Sox baseball game.
    [1. Baseball—Fiction. 2. Grandmothers—Fiction. 3. Magic—Fiction. 4. Ruth, Babe, 1895-1948—Fiction. 5. Jews—United States—Fiction. 6. Chicago (Ill.)—Fiction. 7. Humorous stories.] I. Davis, Jack E., ill.
PZ7.G8278 Mw 2001
[Fic]—dc21
                                                                                    2001040102

ISBN 0-448-42550-5   A B C D E F G H I J

Chapter 1

There are a lot of things in this world I don't understand, but two things stump me the most:

(1) Outer space. I mean, how far out does it go, and how could it never end? And if it *does* end, then *how* does it end? And what's beyond the ending?

(2) My Grandma Leah. She's an eighty-eight-year-old lady with white hair. She's only four-foot-ten. She knows nothing about baseball. So how could she hit a ball farther than Sammy Sosa or Mark McGwire?

My name is Zack. I'm a pretty normal kid, but weird things happen to me all the time. There was the day I drank some disappearing ink and became invisible. And the day I started turning into a cat. And the time my grandma came to visit us and started getting younger and younger till she was a little girl. Well, you get the idea.

Anyway, I live in New York. I'm ten and a half and I'm in the fifth grade at the Horace Hyde-White School for Boys. My parents are divorced, and I spend about half the time with my dad.

I go to Chicago to visit my Grandma Leah at least twice a year. Usually, I go with my dad. This time, he was too busy writing an article about toadstools for *Mushroom World Magazine*, so I went alone on the plane. Grandma picked me up at the airport, and we took a cab to her apartment.

Grandma Leah's apartment is on a high

floor of a building right near Belmont Harbor on Lake Michigan. From her terrace you can see all the boats in the harbor and way out on Lake Michigan. From the roof of her building you can practically see Europe.

As soon as we got to her apartment, Grandma Leah insisted that I have some lunch. I had just eaten lunch on the plane, but I ate again. When Grandma Leah wants you to eat, you might as well eat, because you're going to end up doing it anyway. One thing that Grandma and I always do together is look through old photo albums. She shows me stuff that belonged to my dad when he was a boy. Or stuff that belonged to my Grandpa Sam when he was alive. Grandpa Sam was a big sports fan like me.

So after I finished my grilled-cheese sandwich, Grandma said, "I have something to show you." Grandma went to her room and brought back an old shoebox. I was hoping it might be full of my dad's baseball-card collection.

"I came across this box when I was cleaning my closet," said Grandma Leah as she opened the box. "There's all sorts of—Ouch!" Grandma Leah jumped like she'd gotten an electric shock.

"Grandma," I said, "are you OK?"

"I suppose so," she said. "I don't know what that was. Maybe some…what-do-you-call-it? Static electricity. Here." She handed me the shoebox. "Maybe you'll find something you like."

There were no baseball cards. But there were lots of interesting things. Old programs to Chicago White Sox ball games. Tickets to a Chicago Bears football game signed by quarterback Sid Luckman. An old baseball signed by Chicago Cubs players Andy Pafko, Phil Cavarretta, and Bill Nicholson. An old tennis ball signed by

somebody whose name I couldn't make out.

Also in the box was a strange-looking keychain. It had a tiny metal baseball bat attached to it. The keychain was broken and so tarnished it looked almost black.

"What's that keychain, Grandma?" I asked.

"Your Grandpa Sam bought it at an auction. It belonged to a famous person in sports. Babe Ruth. Do you know the name? He was popular in the old days."

"Are you *kidding* me?" I screamed. "This keychain belonged to Babe Ruth? Grandma Leah, of course I know who Babe Ruth was. He's only the most famous baseball player who ever lived! The greatest home-run hitter, the greatest... This keychain must be worth a fortune!"

"Really?" she said. "It doesn't even look like real gold. It's so tarnished. Let me shine it up for you."

Grandma took the old keychain into the kitchen. She got out a polishing cloth and went to work on it. As soon as she started rubbing it, something weird happened. It started glowing. It was a soft blue glow, like the fire on a gas stove.

"This little bat is quite pretty when you shine it up," said Grandma.

She took the little bat off the keychain and put it on a necklace chain she was wearing. When she did, the soft blue glow seemed to surround her for a moment. Then it faded. Grandma Leah frowned and shook her head.

"Grandma," I said. "What's wrong?"

"I don't know," she said. "I feel a little funny." She sat down on her reclining chair. But she didn't stay there long. She blinked a few times, the way you do when a flashbulb pops in front of your eyes. And then she got up.

"You know what I'd really like to do?" she

said. She was rubbing her hands together and smiling in an excited way.

"Take a nap?" I said. Grandma often takes what she calls "a little snooze" after lunch.

"No no," she said. "Go to the park and hit some baseballs."

I stared at her as if she were crazy.

"You're kidding me," I said.

"Oh no, I'm quite serious. I'd really like to go to the park and smack that old pill around. Just let me change into more comfortable shoes."

And so, Grandma and I went to the park to "smack that old pill around." We started to play, but it was pretty obvious she didn't know the first thing about baseball. She couldn't catch. She couldn't throw. She couldn't run. I gave her a bat and got ready to throw her a pitch. She looked pretty stiff and uncomfortable holding the

bat. A couple of kids stopped to watch. They were whispering and laughing. I knew that they were making fun of her batting stance. I showed her how to stand and how to hold the bat. Then I threw her an easy pitch.

Grandma squinted at the ball as if she wasn't quite sure what she was supposed to do. But then she swung.

The crack of her bat sounded like a rifle shot. The ball went soaring into the air. We both watched it go. The kids who were making fun of her watched, too. Their mouths were open.

"Did I do it right?" asked Grandma Leah.

"Are you kidding me?" I said. "Grandma, that was amazing! Try it again."

I threw her another slow, easy pitch. She smacked it three hundred feet. It cracked off a branch of a huge oak tree and disappeared. I couldn't believe what I was seeing. Neither could the kids who were watching.

"Oh my," said Grandma Leah, "I'm so sorry, Zack. If you can't find that ball, I'll buy you another one."

"Don't worry about it, Grandma," I said. I trotted off to look for the ball. I poked around in some bushes, but I didn't see it.

"Any luck, dear?" she called.

I looked back at my grandma. She was in the batter's crouch, taking a few practice swings. She really looked like a pro now. Weird! What was going on?

I found the ball and headed back toward Grandma. I threw her another pitch. Again, Grandma knocked it at least three hundred feet.

"I don't know what's come over me," Grandma said.

Suddenly I had a feeling that I knew. The little baseball bat charm from the shoebox. The weird blue glow around Grandma Leah when she put it on. I bet it was the bat charm that gave her these amazing powers. Grandma Leah has no patience with weird stuff. She doesn't even like to hear about it. I decided not to say anything. Instead, I tried a little experiment.

I asked to borrow Grandma's necklace and put it around my own neck. I picked up the bat and Grandma threw me a pitch. She had a lot of trouble getting the ball anywhere near me. Eventually I got one where I wanted it. I swung with all my might. The ball went about ten feet and plopped to the ground. I asked her to try it again. When I finally got another pitch I could hit, it went only twenty feet. The necklace wasn't doing anything for me. In fact, I was batting worse than usual.

I just don't get it. If a weird thing is going to happen to anybody, it usually happens to me. Did this mean the bat charm wasn't magic? Or did it mean the magic only worked on Grandma? It seemed really unfair to waste home run-hitting powers on my grandma, who couldn't care less about baseball.

Then I had another idea. Maybe the reason Babe Ruth's tiny bat hadn't worked for me was that it had lost its powers. Grandma had hit three home run–type hits. Genies usually give you only three wishes. Maybe the little bat's powers were already used up.

I gave the necklace back to my grandma. I threw her another pitch. She smacked it so hard, it sailed straight over the trees and into Lake Michigan. Well, there went *that* theory. The baseball charm *was* magic. I was sure of it now. But it looked like it only worked for my grandma. Rats!

I wasn't about to wade into the water to look for the ball, so we went home. Grandma Leah cooked a nice dinner with some of her famous chicken soup with matzoh balls. I made a big fuss over how amazingly she had hit the ball. But it seemed to mean so little to her that I finally just dropped the subject.

The next day we had tickets to see the Chicago White Sox play the Boston Red Sox at Comiskey Park. I live in New York and I love the Yankees, but I also love the White Sox.

I don't know why that is, exactly. Partly it's that the White Sox are in Chicago where my Grandma Leah lives. Partly it's that my dad grew up in Chicago and he loved the White Sox when *he* was a boy.

The White Sox had gotten off to a great start this season, and everybody started talking World Series. But then their hitting fell way off. They started losing games. Right now it looked like they weren't even going to make the play-offs. There were only two games left in the regular season. If the White Sox could win even one against the Red Sox, they'd be in the play-offs. If not, the Red Sox would. I was really hoping the White Sox could pull it off. But they were in a horrible slump.

The guys sitting next to us were White Sox fans. But they kept saying how nothing short of magic could save the team. Little did they know that weird magic stuff was about to happen. Stuff so weird, I wouldn't have believed it myself if I wasn't there. Except that I was.

Chapter 2

It was a beautiful sunny day. The kind where everything looks like it was cleaned and polished. To shield her face from the sun, Grandma Leah had worn a big straw hat. She also wore the necklace with Babe Ruth's little bat on it. She said it might bring the White Sox good luck.

Grandma didn't bring her knitting with her like she usually does. Instead, the minute we took our seats in the stadium, Grandma Leah started asking silly questions. Like "Which one is first base—the one on the left or the one on the right?" And "It's so warm out—why is everybody wearing a glove?" And "Why is that man squatting behind home plate? Can't they get him a chair?"

The guys sitting next to us thought Grandma was a riot. "She's a lot more entertaining than this game," said one of them. It was hard to argue with him.

The game was terrible. The White Sox were hitting worse than ever. They lost 9 to 2. What the Sox needed was a really good hitter. At the end of the game, we walked down to the dugout area.

The dugout is at the edge of the field. It's where the players sit when they're not playing. I saw the White Sox manager and asked him to sign my scorecard.

"You have good fielding, sir," I said. "But if you'll pardon my saying so, my *grandma* here could hit better than most of the guys who batted today."

The manager smiled a tired smile.

"I'm not trying to insult your team, sir," I said. "My grandma *could* hit better than most of the guys who batted today. If you think I'm kidding, give her a try."

"Hey, Jack," the manager yelled to a pitcher who was headed for the clubhouse. "The way you pitched today, I bet you couldn't strike out this kid's grandma!"

"Oh, stuff it," said the pitcher.

The manager seemed annoyed.

"What did you say?" asked the manager.

"I said stuff it," the pitcher answered.

"OK, Jack," said the manager. "Before I was kidding. Now I'm serious. I want you to strike out this kid's grandma."

"Right," said the pitcher. He kept on going toward the clubhouse. The manager got really mad then.

"Hey, Jack!" shouted the manager. "Didn't you hear me? When I said pitch to this kid's grandma, I meant it!"

"Give me a break, Coach," said the pitcher. He looked at Grandma and tipped his cap. "No offense, ma'am, but I'm not pitching to no old lady."

"I'm not an old lady yet, dear," said Grandma Leah to the pitcher. "I'm only eighty-eight."

"I'm not pitching to no eighty-eight-year-old lady," said the pitcher.

"I'm not pitching to *any* eighty-eight-year-old lady," Grandma Leah corrected him.

"How'd you like a five-hundred-dollar fine?" asked the manager.

"I'll *pitch* to her," said the pitcher.

"What do you want me to do, dear?" Grandma whispered to me.

"Hit the ball when he throws it," I said.

I handed her a bat and led her to home plate. "Just like you did yesterday."

"What if I lose their ball?" she whispered.

"They don't care," I said. "They have lots of balls here."

"Oh, I didn't know that," she said.

I gently removed Grandma Leah's straw hat. I took off my White Sox cap and placed it carefully on her head.

The manager grabbed a catcher's mitt. He put on a catcher's mask and squatted down behind the plate. I stood not far from Grandma. In back of the manager, off to the left side, so I could coach her.

The pitcher looked at Grandma Leah. Then he shook his head in disgust and threw. The pitch sped toward the plate at about seventy miles an hour. It landed in the manager's mitt with a loud *thwock*. Then Grandma Leah swung her bat.

"Strike one!" called the manager.

"I *know* you want me to strike one," said Grandma. "That's what I'm trying to do."

The manager looked at me with raised eyebrows. I shrugged.

"She's not used to major-league pitching, sir," I said.

Then I walked up to Grandma Leah. "Grandma, start your swing just as he lets the ball go, OK?"

"All right, dear," she said.

The pitcher wound up for his second pitch. He was just about to throw it when Grandma Leah swung her bat. The ball hit the mitt with another loud *thwock*.

"Strike two!" called the manager.

I snuck back and whispered: "That time, Grandma, you swung a little too early. Start your swing just as he lets the ball go, OK?"

"All right, dear," she said.

The pitcher went into his windup a third

time. He looked at my eighty-eight-year-old grandma standing at the plate. So did I. I noticed something strange around her hands and arms. A bluish glow. And then the pitcher released the ball.

The ball smoked in. It must have been going ninety miles per hour. Grandma Leah swung with all her might. There was no doubt from the *whock* of her bat. She'd gotten hold of this one. The ball shot up, up, up into the air. It scattered a flock of pigeons. It streaked out over right field, out over the upper deck. It went over the roof of Comiskey Park and clear out of the stadium.

"About like that?" asked Grandma Leah.

"Just exactly like that," I replied.

The pitcher's jaw dropped. The manager's eyes grew wide. He took off his mask and looked at me suspiciously.

"OK, kid," he said. "What's going on here? Who's this lady you're calling

Grandma Leah? And how old is she really?"

"She really is my Grandma Leah, sir," I said proudly. I put my arm around her. "And she really is eighty-eight years old."

"Yeah, right," he said. He turned to my grandma. "What did you do, sis, play Triple-A ball or what?"

"Triple-A?" said Grandma Leah. "Oh my, no. I'm not even a member of the Automobile Club."

"Then where'd she learn to hit like that?" he asked me.

"In the park yesterday, sir," I said. And then I had a really awesome idea. "Hey, how about using her in tomorrow's game against the Red Sox?"

"Yeah, right," said the manager.

"I'm serious, sir," I said. "Why don't you use her?"

"Because. I can't play an eighty-eight-year-old lady, OK?"

"Why can't you?" I asked.

"Why can't I?" he repeated. "Because I can't, that's why. Look, kid. Your granny hit one ball out of the park, OK? I admit it was a good shot. But it was a fluke. She'll never be able to do it again."

"Grandma," I said, "would you mind hitting a few more balls?"

"Would it please you, Zack?" she asked.

"It would please me a *lot*," I said.

"All right, dear," she said.

I positioned her back in the batter's box. Then I got out of the way. The pitcher wasn't at all happy, but he didn't want to pay a five-hundred-dollar fine either.

I noticed the strange bluish glow had spread all over Grandma Leah now. Nobody but me seemed to notice. The pitcher wound up and sent a curve ball zooming toward the plate.

"Swing, Grandma!" I yelled.

Grandma Leah swung a mighty swing. There was another loud crack of wood against leather. The ball streaked high into the air, like it had been shot out of a cannon. It sailed over left field. It plopped softly into the upper deck.

"Home run!" I shouted, "Way to go, Grandma! Do it again!"

The pitcher looked embarrassed and angry. I didn't blame him. It didn't do much for your image to have eighty-eight-year-old grandmas hitting homers off you. He wound up and threw a fast ball toward the plate. It was low and outside.

"Go for it, Grandma!" I yelled.

Grandma Leah went for it. Her bat smacked it hard. It went whizzing over the right-field wall.

"Three back-to-back homers!" I shouted. "Yee-hah! Do it again, Grandma!"

The pitcher clenched his teeth. He glared

at my grandma. He wound up again. He threw a sinker.

"Swing, Grandma!" I shouted.

Grandma Leah swung. Her bat seemed to crackle with blue electricity. She sent a line drive screaming back toward the pitcher's mound at about a hundred miles an hour. The pitcher hit the dirt to get out of its way. The ball hit the center-field wall like a bullet. It tore a hole through the padding. It buried itself in the concrete.

"Is that an inside-the-park home run, sir, or a ground-rule double?" I asked.

The manager covered his face with his hands.

"Want to see her do it again, sir?"

"I don't think that'll be necessary," said the manager from behind his hands.

"Does that mean you'll use her tomorrow against the Red Sox, sir?" I asked excitedly.

He sighed deeply. Then he thought it

over. "I don't know. I just don't know. I mean I don't even know where I'd play her. What position does she play?"

That threw me. If Grandma Leah had to try out for any position in the field we were dead. From playing with her in the park I knew she couldn't catch. She couldn't throw. She couldn't run. She didn't even know one base from the other. Fortunately, in the American League they use a Designated Hitter to bat for the pitcher. A Designated Hitter doesn't ever have to play in the field.

"How about Designated Hitter?" I said.

He thought that over. Then he sighed.

"You know," he said, "they're probably going to send me to the loony bin for this. But you seem to be serious about your grandma playing tomorrow. And I'm willing to put her in as Designated Hitter."

"Whoopee!" I yelled. "Hey, Grandma,

how'd you like to play tomorrow against the Boston Red Sox?"

"Oh my, no, dear," she said. She put down her bat and walked over to me. "We've seen one baseball game today and that is quite enough for a while."

The manager dropped his hands.

"You don't *want* to play?" he said.

"No, dear," said Grandma. "But thanks for asking."

"Why don't you?" asked the manager.

"Well, for one thing," she said, "I have a big brisket to cook tomorrow. And that will take nearly all day."

"I don't believe this," said the manager.

"Grandma," I said, "this man is willing to let you play ball tomorrow with the Chicago White Sox! Do you know what an honor that is? Do you know how many people would give their right *arm* for a chance to play ball with the Chicago White Sox?"

"How could they play ball if they gave away their right arm?" Grandma asked.

"I don't believe this," said the manager.

He seemed really disappointed. I led Grandma Leah away from home plate for a little conference.

"Grandma Leah," I said, "couldn't you do this just once for me? Please? If you don't like it, you'll never have to do it again. I promise. On my word of honor."

"If I play tomorrow, Zack," she said, "who'll cook the brisket?"

Grandma Leah was a great cook, but there were other great cooks. And nobody could hit the long ball the way that she could.

"Maybe Aunt Naomi could come over and cook it if we ask her to," I said. "Couldn't you just please, please do this for me, Grandma Leah? Couldn't you, please?"

"Let me think this over a minute and then I'll decide," she said.

I looked over at the manager and shrugged. I held up two crossed fingers.

Grandma Leah wrinkled her forehead, thinking. Then she put her arm around me.

"Zack dear, I'd do anything in the world to make you happy," she said. "Does it really mean that much to you?"

"It does," I said. "I've never known anybody who played for a major-league team. And Dad would be proud of you, too."

"Well," she sighed, "then I guess the brisket can wait!"

"Yippee!" I shouted. I threw my arms around her and hugged her.

"Does that mean she'll do it?" asked the manager.

"Just for the one game, dear," said Grandma Leah.

"Game time is one-thirty, Grandma Leah," he said. "But I want you here at noon for batting practice."

Chapter 3

That night I asked Grandma if I could look at the necklace with Babe Ruth's little bat on it. I looked it over carefully from all sides. I wondered if some kind of supernatural energy from Babe Ruth himself had rubbed off on her. It was a pretty weird idea. But no weirder than the way my grandma could hit now.

As I was holding the necklace, I noticed something. A kind of fog was seeping into my room from under the door. A glowing blue fog. As I watched it, the fog began to form a shape. The shape of a person. The shape of…a ghost!

The glowing shape slid toward me. Yikes!

I tried to yell for my grandma. But all that came out was a squeak.

The glowing shape became a man. A pretty fat man in an old New York Yankees uniform.

"M…Mr. Ruth?" I called out. "Is that you?"

"Yeah, kid. Sorry if I scared you. How's it going?"

"Wow, this…Wow!" I said. "This is unbelievable! I can't tell you how honored I am to meet you, sir. I'm a really *huge* fan."

"Thanks, kid," he said. "You seem like a real nice kid. And I like your grandma, too. She swings a pretty mean bat, for a youngster."

"A youngster?" I said. "Grandma Leah is eighty-eight."

"Well, I'm a hundred and six," said the Babe. "To me she's a youngster."

"I was wondering, Mr. Ruth, sir," I said. "Does Grandma's home-run hitting have something to do with that little bat on her necklace?"

"Oh, maybe a little," he said, smiling. "She *is* going to play in the game tomorrow against the Red Sox, though, right?"

"Yeah," I said. "Why do you ask?"

"I really need her to play," said the Babe.

"What do you mean?"

"It's a long story, kid," said the Babe. "It started when the Red Sox sold me to the Yankees without even asking if I wanted to go. I wasn't too thrilled about that. Ever since then, well, the Red Sox have never won a World Series."

"Then the famous Babe Ruth curse is *true*?" I said. "Amazing!"

"Yeah. And if your grandma hits some homers tomorrow, maybe we can keep this thing going awhile longer."

"So you want my grandma to help you keep the Red Sox out of the play-offs for another year?"

"Well," said the Babe, "a ghost can't do everything by himself, you know."

He started fading. He raised his arm and waved. "Good luck, kid," he said. "See you tomorrow at the game." The glowing shape dissolved and vanished.

I couldn't believe it! Babe Ruth—*the* Babe Ruth—was asking my grandma for help in a baseball game! I just hoped she could pull it off.

Chapter 4

I don't know how they did it, but by the time we brought Grandma to Comiskey Park at noon the next day, the White Sox had a uniform for her. They gave her number 88, for her age. The uniform fit her perfectly. OK, maybe not perfectly. The pant legs were a little long. But we rolled them up and she looked fine. And of course she wore Babe Ruth's bat on her necklace.

"How do I look?" she asked me.

"Very cool, Grandma," I said. "Like a real pro."

We went down to the dugout. They let me sit with Grandma on the bench. The other players were very nice to her. One of them offered her some chewing tobacco. She said no and warned them about the dangers of tobacco.

It was a hot, sunny day. Hotter than yesterday. The game started. It was the White Sox's last chance to make the play-offs. If they lost, it was all over till next year. The Red Sox would go to the play-offs, and Babe Ruth would be really disappointed.

Unfortunately, the Red Sox got off to an early lead. By the top of the sixth inning they were winning 7 to 3. I went to talk to the White Sox manager.

"Looks like we could use a few runs here, sir," I said. "Why don't you give my grandma a chance to bat?"

"OK," said the manager. "But not now."

In the seventh and eighth innings

neither team got a man on base. Grandma Leah was growing bored.

"When will this be over, dear?" she whispered to me. "It's not so interesting. And I want to get home and start cooking our dinner."

"There's just one more inning, Grandma," I said.

"I thought they wanted me to play," she said. She sounded disappointed.

"Yeah," I said, "so did I."

Going into the last of the ninth, the score was still Red Sox 7, White Sox 3. Then the Red Sox pitcher walked four straight men, forcing in a run. It was now 7 to 4, with bases loaded and no outs. I began to get excited. But the next man up popped out. And the next one grounded out. And now there was only one more chance to win the game.

"Please, sir," I begged the manager. "Put my grandma in."

"I want to," he said. "I really do. I'm just afraid we'll get laughed off the field."

I didn't know what to tell him. I could hardly say that the ghost of Babe Ruth was helping her. Then I had an idea.

"Sir," I said, "my grandma's only four-foot-ten."

"So?"

"So that's a very narrow strike zone. If she just stands there and doesn't swing, she'll get a walk. That will force in a run."

"You want me to use her just because she has a narrow strike zone?" he asked.

"It's been done before," I said, "You remember a former White Sox manager named Bill Veeck? When he managed the St. Louis Browns, he once put in a midget as a pinch hitter."

"Really?" he said.

"It was in a game with the Detroit Tigers in 1951," I said. "The midget's name was Eddie Gaedel. He was three-foot-seven."

"Batter up!" yelled the umpire.

The manager turned. He looked at Grandma Leah on the bench in the dugout.

"OK," he said. "She can bat for Johnson."

"Fantastic!" I said. "Hey, Grandma! He's going to let you bat!"

"Zack," she whispered, "I'm afraid I won't know what to do."

"Do exactly what I tell you," I said. "Promise?"

"I promise," she whispered.

Then Grandma took her makeup bag out of her purse. As soon as she put on some fresh lipstick, she got up to bat.

Chapter 5

"**W**ait, Grandma Leah!" said the manager. "When you get up to the plate, take the walk."

Grandma Leah frowned. "In other words," she said, "you want me to walk to the plate?"

"Yes," said the manager. "And when you get there, take the walk."

"Once I get there, where do you want me to walk?" she asked.

"Let *me* explain it to her, sir," I said. "Grandma, once you get to the plate he doesn't want you to swing. He wants you to let the pitcher *walk* you. Do you know what that means?"

"Of *course* I know what that means," she said. She looked hurt. "I may be eighty-eight, but I don't need anybody to *walk* me. I can still do it myself."

"Grandma Leah," I said. "Being walked means you let the pitcher throw four balls. Then you take your base."

"Where do I take it?" she said.

"You don't take it anywhere," I said. "You just walk to it. If the pitcher throws four balls, the batter automatically goes to first."

"What if he throws only *one* ball?" she asked. "But he throws it four times?"

"Same thing," I said.

"Batter up!" yelled the umpire.

The fans were beginning to get restless. They began clapping and shouting. Some of them were booing.

"Please go to the plate, Grandma Leah," I said.

"And whatever you do, don't swing your bat," said the manager.

"All right," said Grandma Leah.

I handed her a bat and a batting helmet. She climbed out of the dugout and walked to the plate. The manager and I followed her out there.

"NOW BATTING FOR JOHNSON..." boomed the P.A. system. It echoed through the whole stadium. "THE DESIGNATED HIT-TER...NUMBER 88...GRANDMA LEAH...!"

"Who the heck is *this*?" asked the plate umpire.

"Our new Designated Hitter," said the manager. "Her name is Grandma Leah. She's on today's roster."

"What are you trying to do?" said the ump. "Put her in because she's short and has a narrow strike zone?"

The manager didn't answer.

The fans were really starting to boo. It was making me nervous. It didn't seem to bother Grandma Leah at all. She didn't realize they were booing *her*.

"You can't put somebody in to pinch-hit just because they're short," said the ump. "It's never been done before."

"You want to bet?" I said. "Bill Veeck did it in 1951 with a three-foot-seven-inch midget named Eddie Gaedel."

"Really?" said the ump. "Well, then, I guess it's OK. Batter up!"

Grandma Leah faced the Red Sox pitcher. She stood at the plate in a very ladylike way. She held her bat high in the air. She smiled at the pitcher and waved.

The pitcher stared at her a moment in disbelief. Then he shook his head and went into his windup. He let one go with terrific speed. It was a knuckleball, high and outside.

"Ball one!" yelled the ump.

Some of the fans cheered.

"Good eye, Grandma!" I called.

"What, dear?" she said.

"Good eye," I said. "It's what you say when a batter lets a bad pitch go by without swinging at it."

"Oh," she said. "Thank you."

The pitcher adjusted the bill of his cap. He went into his windup a second time. The ball came whizzing in. It was a curve ball. Low and inside.

"Ball two!" yelled the ump.

The fans cheered again.

"Do I have two good eyes now, dear?"

"Yes, Grandma," I said.

"Remember, don't swing!" called the manager.

The pitcher stared at Grandma Leah. He went into his windup. He let the third ball go. It came in right over the center of the plate, waist high. A perfect pitch. I groaned. I knew what she could have done with it.

"Stee-rike!" yelled the ump.

The fans booed.

"Oh, was I supposed to strike at that one, dear?" Grandma Leah asked me. She looked worried.

"No, Grandma," I said. "You're doing great."

"Don't strike at anything!" called the manager. "Just stand absolutely still!"

The next pitch was another perfect pitch. Waist high. Just catching the outside corner of the plate.

"Strike two!" yelled the ump.

The White Sox fans realized they were one strike away from defeat. One strike away from not getting into the play-offs. They booed even louder.

The next pitch was low and inside.

"Ball three!" yelled the ump.

The fans cheered.

"Way to go, Grandma!" I called.

"Is it now that I'm supposed to take my base somewhere, dear?" she asked me.

"Wait for one more ball, Grandma," I said. "Then take your base."

"And don't swing at it, whatever you do!" called the manager.

"All right, dear," she called back.

Grandma Leah now had a full count of three balls and two strikes. If she didn't swing at the next pitch and it was a ball, she'd go to first. That would force in a run. But if she didn't swing and it was a strike, the game would be over. And with it the White Sox chances of making the play-offs. I was so nervous I couldn't stand it.

In front of me a glowing blue fog began to take shape. The blue fog became Babe Ruth. Nobody else seemed to notice.

"Hiya, kid," said Babe Ruth. "Howya doin'?"

"Not bad, Mr. Ruth," I said. "How about you?"

"Can't complain," said Babe Ruth. "I think I should tell you. The next pitch is going to be a beauty. It'll be another perfect pitch."

"You're sure of that?" I asked.

"Trust me," said Babe Ruth.

The pitcher went into his windup.

"Swing, Grandma, swing!" I shouted.

"No, don't swing!" yelled the manager.

"Swing with all your might!" I screamed.

Grandma Leah began to glow with a strange bluish glow.

The pitcher released the ball. It smoked in at a hundred miles per hour.

Grandma swung the bat with all her might. The sound of the ball hitting her bat was like an explosion.

The ball went soaring into the air over center field at a very high angle. If she'd hit it at a lower angle, it would have been out of the park. But she'd hit it almost straight up. And now it was nearly out of sight in the sky above us.

The fans made lots of noise. Outfielders don't often miss pop flies. But there was a chance the Red Sox center fielder might lose this ball in the sun. And then Grandma Leah could maybe make it to first. But only if she started running. So far she was standing still.

"Run, Grandma, run!" I screamed.

"Run!" yelled the manager. He was jumping up and down.

"Run!" shouted Babe Ruth. But no one heard him except me.

Grandma Leah turned back to look at me in confusion.

"Where should I run to, dear?" she asked.

The ball was now completely out of sight. The crowd was roaring.

"To first base!" I screamed.

"Is first base the one on the left or the one on the right, dear?" she asked.

"On the right!" I shouted.

"On the right!" shouted the manager. His face was bright red.

"On the right!" shouted Babe Ruth. But again no one saw or heard him.

The center fielder began dropping back. He was trying to guess where the ball would reappear. The fans were screaming "Run! Run! Run! Run! Run! Run!"

"So, in other words," said Grandma Leah, "I just run to the right until I get to that little white pillow on the ground there. Is that it?"

"Yes!" I screamed. "Run, Grandma, run!"

"Run, sweetheart, run!" Babe shouted.

I thought *I* was going to have a heart attack too. Along with all the fans in Comiskey Park.

The center fielder kept dropping back until he backed right into the center-field wall.

Grandma Leah took off toward first base at a slow trot. Her arms were pumping. As I said before, she's four-foot-ten. Her legs are short, and it was the best she could do.

The ball reappeared. It was a tiny speck in the sky. It began to fall earthward.

"Faster, Grandma!" I yelled.

"I'm running as fast as I can!" called Grandma Leah. She was puffing hard. But she was now only a quarter of the way to first. As I said before, she was a lot better batter than a runner.

With his glove hand extended, the center fielder watched the ball fall toward him.

Chapter 6

Grandma Leah was a third of the way to first base. She was puffing so hard I was getting worried. The first-base coach was frantically waving her on with both hands. It looked like he was conducting a symphony.

When the ball was almost upon him, the center fielder leaped six feet into the air.

But it was way over his head, and he missed it by a foot. The ball went sailing into the lower deck in center field. The fans went absolutely crazy. They were screaming and yelling and throwing things up into the air.

"Home run!" I screamed. "Way to go, Grandma Leah!" I tried to high-five Babe Ruth, but my hand went right through his foggy blue one.

"GRAND SLAM HOMER...FOR NUMBER 88...GRANDMA LEAH!" boomed the P.A. system.

The man on third raced across home plate. Followed by the man on second. Followed by the man on first. Poor Grandma! She'd finally reached first and was on her way to second. She was huffing and puffing so hard, I didn't see how she'd ever get around all the bases.

"Well, kid," said the Babe. "The Red Sox have been defeated, and your grandma has saved the day. Looks like my work here is done. Take it easy, and tell your grandma thanks from the Babe." He gave Grandma Leah a thumbs-up, which she never saw, and then he dissolved in a haze of blue fog.

Grandma Leah was still on her way to second. She was puffing harder than ever. Five minutes later she shuffled across home plate. The game was finally over. Thanks to Grandma, the White Sox had won it, 8 to 7! I hugged her.

"You're a hero, Grandma!" I shouted.

"Grandma Leah," said the manager, "you disobeyed my orders. But you did put us into the play-offs. So I have to thank you."

All the White Sox gave Grandma high fives. Sports reporters and TV camera crews surrounded her. She seemed to enjoy the attention.

"Grandma Leah," said the reporter from Fox-TV, "where did you ever learn to hit like that?"

"My grandson Zack taught me how in the park yesterday," said Grandma.

"Grandma Leah," said the reporter from

ABC-TV, "why did you swing when the manager told you not to?"

"Because my grandson told me to," she replied. "And he knows more about baseball than anybody in the world."

"Grandma Leah," said the reporter from NBC-TV, "you've just been voted the Most Valuable Player of today's game. How do you feel about that?"

"Well," she said, "it's nice to be recognized. But I think everybody on the team did a lovely job."

So that's how my Grandma Leah got the Chicago White Sox into the play-offs. It was definitely with Babe Ruth's help. But mostly it was Grandma herself. Wherever he is, I think the Babe is as proud of her as I am. I never saw Babe Ruth again. I like to think he's busy helping other kids' grandmas get onto professional baseball teams.

Grandma let me take the Babe Ruth bat charm back to New York, but it didn't work for me there either. I don't mind anymore. I mean, not that much. At least it worked for Grandma.

The same day she was voted Rookie of the Year, Grandma announced her retirement from professional baseball. She said it was to spend more time with her family, but at her press conference she whispered the real reason to me.

"Frankly, Zack," she said, "I find baseball rather boring. It's much too slow a game for me. Also, I hate to say this, but the other White Sox players aren't very good hitters. And it just wasn't fair to expect me to carry the whole team on my back."

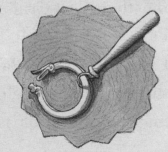

What else happens to Zack?
Find out in

Greenish Eggs and Dinosaurs

"Something is happening," I whispered. "Something weird."

There was a tapping sound from inside the egg.

"Did you hear that?" I said. "There's something *alive* inside that thing!"

"Nonsense," said Dad. "Nothing could have survived being cooked in the microwave."

The tapping sound got louder. Then the entire top of the egg popped off it. Something green and slimy poked its head out and looked at us with glowing red eyes. It had a long pointed snout, and when it opened its mouth I saw rows of sharp, tiny teeth. Its skin was scaly and slimy and green.

"Holy guacamole!" I said. "A dinosaur!"

THE ZACK FILES™

OUT-OF-THIS-WORLD FAN CLUB!

Looking for even more info on all the strange, otherworldly happenings going on in *The Zack Files*? Get the inside scoop by becoming a member of *The Zack Files* Out-Of-This-World Fan Club! Just send in the form below and we'll send you your *Zack Files* Out-Of-This-World Fan Club kit including an official fan club membership card, a really cool *Zack Files* magnet, and a newsletter featuring excerpts from Zack's upcoming paranormal adventures, supernatural news from around the world, puzzles, and more! And as a member you'll continue to receive the newsletter six times a year! The best part is—it's all free!

✂ --

☐ Yes! I want to check out *The Zack Files*
　 Out-Of-This-World Fan Club!

name: _____ age: ____

address: _____

city/town: _____ state: ___ zip: _____

Send this form to: Penguin Putnam Books for
    Young Readers
    Mass Merchandise Marketing
    Dept. ZACK
    345 Hudson Street
    New York, NY 10014